Samuel French Acting Edition

I0591787

Mercy

by Adam Szymkowicz

SAMUELFRENCH.COM   SAMUELFRENCH.CO.UK

FOR PRODUCTION ENQUIRIES

UNITED STATES AND CANADA
Info@SamuelFrench.com
1-866-598-8449

UNITED KINGDOM AND EUROPE
Plays@SamuelFrench.co.uk
020-7255-4302

Each title is subject to availability from Samuel French, depending
upon country of performance. Please be aware that *MERCY* may not be
licensed by Samuel French in your territory. Professional and amateur
producers should contact the nearest Samuel French office or licensing
partner to verify availability.

MUSIC USE NOTE

Licensees are solely responsible for obtaining formal written permission from copyright owners to use copyrighted music in the performance of this play and are strongly cautioned to do so. If no such permission is obtained by the licensee, then the licensee must use only original music that the licensee owns and controls. Licensees are solely responsible and liable for all music clearances and shall indemnify the copyright owners of the play(s) and their licensing agent, Samuel French, against any costs, expenses, losses and liabilities arising from the use of music by licensees. Please contact the appropriate music licensing authority in your territory for the rights to any incidental music.

IMPORTANT BILLING AND CREDIT REQUIREMENTS

If you have obtained performance rights to this title, please refer to your licensing agreement for important billing and credit requirements.

MERCY premiered at New Jersey Repertory Theater in Long Branch, New Jersey on June 14, 2018; Artistic Director SuzAnne Barabas, Executive Director Gabor Barabas. It was directed by Gail Winar with assistant direction by Jane E. Huber, sets by Jessica Parks, lights by Jill Nagle, sound by Merek Royce Press, and costume design by Patricia E. Doherty. The technical director was Brian Snyder, the master electrician was James Lockhart, and the box office manager and assistant to the Artistic Director was Alli Angelou. The production stage manager was Kristin Pfeifer and assistant stage manager was Adam von Pier. The cast was as follows:

IAN SANDERS	Christopher Daftsios
WALTER MARKS	Dan Grimaldi
BRENDA JAMES	Nandita Shenoy
ORVILLE MARKS	Jacob A. Ware
UNDERSTUDY	Chris Price

CHARACTERS

Actors can be any race

ORVILLE MARKS – (30s-40s)
WALTER MARKS – (mid-60s) Orville's father
BRENDA JAMES – (mid-30s-early 40s) Orville's boss
IAN SANDERS – (mid-20s-early 30s)

SETTING

Orville's home (Brooklyn), Orville's work (Manhattan), a bar
(Manhattan), a church basement (Manhattan), Ian's apartment
(Manhattan), a hotel room (Manhattan)
These can be minimally suggested

TIME

The Present

AUTHOR'S NOTE

Ian's homosexuality should be a surprise to the audience as much as
possible.

SPECIAL THANKS

In no particular order to SuzAnne, Gabe, Gail, and the wonderful
cast and crew of the NJ Rep production, Joel Stone, John and Rhoda
Szymkowicz, Seth Glewen, the Gersh Agency, Tish Dace, the Juilliard
School, Kristen Palmer, Wallace Szymkowicz, Barefoot Theatre
Company, Scott Illingworth, Mike Carlsen, John Doman, Kathleen
Littlefield, Francisco Solorzano, Ashley Marie Ortiz, Primary Stages,
Michelle Bossy, Brian Hutchison, Keith Buterbaugh, J. Robert Spencer,
Susan Blackwell, Patrice Bell, Bekah Brunstetter, Cheri Magid, Brian
Pracht, Josh Allen, Courtney Baron, Janine Nabers, Molly Smith Metzler,
Rogelio Martinez, Melissa Ross, MCC Theater, Ashlin Halfnight, Alex
Lewin, Ethan McSweeney, Greg Keller, Bob Hogan, Susan Louise
O'Connor, Patch Darragh, Mark Schultz, Stephen Willems, Markus
Potter, Zack Robidas, Dan Grimaldi, Sarah Kate Jackson, Erik Heger,
Oanh Nguyen and the Chance Theater, the Asylum Theater, William
Adamson, Doug Baker, JJ Gatesman, Christina Greer, Sarah O'Connell,
Flux Theatre Ensemble, Wilbury Theater Group, Josh Short, Ben Jolivet,
Christina Saad Wolfskehl, Azuka Theatre, Kevin Glaccum, Mike Dees,
Tim Dugan, Alex Keiper, Bob Lohrman, Kelly O'Donnell, and Marsha
Norman. And to the many, many actors who helped me develop this
play, I am truly grateful.

For Michelle Bossy,
a tireless advocate, a terrific dramaturg, a fantastic director,
and a great friend.

Scene One

*(**ORVILLE** talking to the baby who is in a bassinet or carrier.)*

ORVILLE. It's a good idea, they say, to talk to you, even though you don't know what I'm saying. I wish you would cry. It's not right. People tell me I'm lucky that you're not crying all night and all day, but still, it's not natural not to cry at all. The doctors say there's nothing wrong with you but I don't trust doctors anymore and you shouldn't either.

You could say *something*. Tell me when you're wet or hungry. Just say, "Hey!" Can you say that? Hey! Hey. Say, "Hey!" Hey. Hey. Hey. Hey. Just say it. Like me. Hey. Hey. Hey. Or, you know, something else. I don't have to control you. You could say "Dad." Da-da. Da-da. Dad. Dad. Da-da.

Okay, well, whenever you're ready. Just don't, I mean you don't have to hold back on my account. Too many people are not being themselves around me anymore. Feel free to cry and scream and just let go. Neighbors be damned.

No one expected you to live. You're a miracle, you know that? And you're fine. They say everything is fine. So go ahead and cry your lungs out. God knows you have reason enough.

(Pause.)

No?

(He begins to cry, at first modeling behavior for the baby, and then really getting into it.)

Anhh! Anhh! Anhhh! ANHHH! ANHHH!
ANHHHH! ANHHH! ANHHH! ANHHHH!
ANHHHHHHHHH!

(Blackout.)

Scene Two

(**ORVILLE** *at his desk in an office.* **BRENDA** *approaches.*)

BRENDA. Orville!

ORVILLE. Brenda.

BRENDA. It's great to have you back.

ORVILLE. Thanks.

BRENDA. We missed you.

ORVILLE. Yeah.

BRENDA. I'm sorry about –

ORVILLE. Yeah.

BRENDA. Everything. How's the – um – baby?

ORVILLE. Fine.

BRENDA. What's her name?

ORVILLE. Oh we don't – I mean I don't have one yet.

BRENDA. Oh.

ORVILLE. I'll have to think of one, I guess.

BRENDA. You want suggestions?

ORVILLE. Uh...

BRENDA. Gloria. Ricki. Cicily. Alyssa. Jasmine. Helen?

ORVILLE. Yeah, I don't know.

BRENDA. Louise. Sally. Beverly. Cindy. Antoinette. Lucy. Irina.

ORVILLE. I don't really need suggestions.

BRENDA. I once had a goldfish named Erin.

ORVILLE. Huh.

BRENDA. And a tetra named Tetra.

ORVILLE. *(Being polite.)* That's nice.

BRENDA. Oh, no. Don't name her Tetra.

ORVILLE. Okay.

BRENDA. Good. So you're a single dad now.

ORVILLE. Yeah.

BRENDA. A baby.

ORVILLE. Yup.

BRENDA. I never had – I mean – we couldn't have – so I secretly always hate people who have kids.

ORVILLE. Oh.

BRENDA. But it's hard to hate you.

ORVILLE. Thanks.

BRENDA. Because of what happened.

ORVILLE. Oh.

BRENDA. So I wish you well.

ORVILLE. Thanks.

      (Pause.)

BRENDA. *(In boss mode.)* So how's that cost analysis coming?

ORVILLE. Should have it later today.

BRENDA. Good. Good. So, um also HR wanted to make sure you were seeing someone. You know – to deal with the – uh – grief. If you want them to set something up for you –

ORVILLE. No.

BRENDA. Okay well, I delivered the message.

ORVILLE. Thanks.

BRENDA. Are you already seeing someone?

ORVILLE. No.

BRENDA. Like a therapist I mean, not dating. Ha! Are you dating?

ORVILLE. No.

BRENDA. I guess it's a little soon.

ORVILLE. Yeah.

BRENDA. A counselor might be good though.

ORVILLE. No.

BRENDA. It might help.

ORVILLE. No. I've never done that. I don't like to talk to strangers.

BRENDA. Maybe you have a friend. Do you need a friend?

ORVILLE. Okay, well, I'll email you the report when it's done.

BRENDA. Oh, okay. Well we're all here for you. If you need anything –

ORVILLE. Like what?

BRENDA. I don't know.

ORVILLE. I mean people say that but what does that mean?

BRENDA. Well –

ORVILLE. Are you going to get me coffee? If I say I could use coffee, would you go get coffee?

BRENDA. Well –

ORVILLE. Or do you want me to open up to you and cry on your shoulder.

BRENDA. No, I mean, if you need to leave early or something.

ORVILLE. Oh. That's pretty reasonable actually.

BRENDA. We're here for you. If you need time. If you need, I don't know.

ORVILLE. I'm okay.

BRENDA. I don't think you are.

Scene Three

(**WALTER** *is holding the baby. Enter* **ORVILLE**.)

WALTER. Hey.

ORVILLE. Hey.

WALTER. How was work?

ORVILLE. Fine.

WALTER. You want to hold her?

ORVILLE. *(Backing away.)* No. That's okay. You want a beer?

    (**ORVILLE** *exits to get beer.*)

WALTER. Yeah. We went to Prospect Park today. She helped me hit on the ladies. *(To baby.)* Didn't you?

    (**ORVILLE** *re-enters with two bottles of beer. Hands one to his father.*)

ORVILLE. You used the baby to hit on women?

WALTER. Better than a dog.

ORVILLE. She's not a dog.

WALTER. I said better than a dog. I like the parks here. I got a couple numbers. Young single mothers.

ORVILLE. Okay, that's – I'm happy for you, I guess. You're going to call them?

WALTER. Sure. Why not? Taking care of a baby that isn't mine makes me look like a catch, which, let's face it, I am.

ORVILLE. You've been doing that?

WALTER. What?

ORVILLE. Dating.

WALTER. Sure. The last couple of years.

ORVILLE. Oh.

WALTER. You thought after your mom, I would –

ORVILLE. No.

WALTER. I loved your mother. She was the love of my life. We had forty-three wonderful years together. But she's gone. A man shouldn't stay celibate forever. In fact you should get out there.

ORVILLE. Dad – too soon. Too soon.

WALTER. Okay, maybe a little. But in a couple weeks, a month.

ORVILLE. She was just here, in this house. She was just sleeping next to me.

WALTER. I know it feels that way. It was like that for me with your mother too.

ORVILLE. This is different.

WALTER. I know.

ORVILLE. This was sudden.

WALTER. It doesn't make me miss her any less.

ORVILLE. Yeah. I know. How's it going?

WALTER. What?

ORVILLE. The baby. Did she cry?

WALTER. No. She's been a little angel. I was thinking, we should come up with a temporary name. I mean, if you're not ready to name her, that's fine, but it might help to have something to call her.

ORVILLE. Why?

WALTER. I don't know. It's nice. Anyway, when the ladies come over to coo at her, the first thing they ask is, "What's her name?" I've just been making up names. I think she likes Florence.

ORVILLE. Florence?

WALTER. She smiled almost when I said it.

ORVILLE. She smiled?

WALTER. Well, her mouth kind of moved. It could have been a smile.

ORVILLE. Can she smile?

WALTER. I mean, she wouldn't have learned it from you.

ORVILLE. Are you telling me to cheer up?

WALTER. I wouldn't say that.

ORVILLE. You can call her whatever you want.

WALTER. I don't want to call her something and have her get attached to it and then you decide you hate it.

ORVILLE. I hate Florence.

WALTER. All right. There you go. What do you want to call her?

ORVILLE. I can't do this now.

WALTER. You want to name her after Carrie?

ORVILLE. No. No. We can't do that to her.

WALTER. Okay, well –

ORVILLE. It's not right.

WALTER. Name her after your mother?

ORVILLE. No. I'll name it.

WALTER. Her.

ORVILLE. What?

WALTER. You said "it."

ORVILLE. I did?

WALTER. In some cultures they wait until the kid is old enough to name herself.

ORVILLE. No. I'll do it.

WALTER. I could call her "Pudding" until then.

ORVILLE. Pudding?

WALTER. That makes her smile too.

ORVILLE. We're not calling her Pudding.

WALTER. You got another name?

ORVILLE. *(Thinks.)* No.

WALTER. Okay, well, think about it.

ORVILLE. I will.

WALTER. I'm going out.

ORVILLE. You are?

WALTER. I mean unless – you got it all under control, right?

ORVILLE. Yeah.

WALTER. You sure?

ORVILLE. I can take care of my own kid.

(**WALTER** *goes to give the baby to* **ORVILLE** *but* **ORVILLE** *does not reach out.* **WALTER** *puts her in the bassinet.*)

WALTER. I'll only be a couple of hours, at the most. Call me if you need anything.

ORVILLE. Where are you going?

WALTER. Date.

ORVILLE. Already?

WALTER. Oh, no. Not from today. This is from the internet.

ORVILLE. What do you mean? Are you on Tinder or something?

WALTER. Something. She's a little young for me, but I figure, what the hell. I could help you set up a profile if you want to give it a shot.

ORVILLE. No, that's okay.

WALTER. When you're ready.

ORVILLE. I'm fine.

WALTER. Look, I'll be here in your apartment with you. I'll stick around as long as I can to help out, but eventually –

ORVILLE. What?

WALTER. Eventually, you're going to have to get your shit together again. I'm not trying to give you a hard time. I know you're going through a lot. But this is your kid right here. She needs you.

ORVILLE. I'm right here. I'm taking care of it.

WALTER. Her.

ORVILLE. Go on your date.

WALTER. You sure everything's under control?

ORVILLE. Go.

WALTER. I won't be long. Even if she wants me to stay over.

ORVILLE. Go.

WALTER. I'm going. I'll see if she has a sister for you.

ORVILLE. Don't do that.

WALTER. Okay. Bye, Pudding.

(**WALTER** *kisses her goodbye. He exits.* **ORVILLE**
looks at the baby.)

ORVILLE. Don't look at me like that. I'm trying.
I'll try to pull it together for you. Okay? Okay?

(*Pause.*)

You want to say anything?

(*Pause.*)

You sure?

Scene Four

(In the office. ORVILLE works at his desk. BRENDA watches him. After a while she comes over to his desk.)

BRENDA. Orville.

ORVILLE. Oh, hey.

BRENDA. Can we talk?

ORVILLE. I'm kind of in the middle –

BRENDA. I'd like to have a discussion, not as boss and employee but as friends. I feel like we can do that because we're closer now because of what happened to you. I have more sympathy for you and you're more open and vulnerable.

ORVILLE. Why do you think I'm more open?

BRENDA. Aren't you?

ORVILLE. I could be more closed off.

BRENDA. Oh sure, just not to me. Not anymore. We've evolved. Relationships have to evolve. And I feel like ours is, don't you?

ORVILLE. Uh –

BRENDA. It can evolve more, it can always evolve more, but – can I talk to you?

ORVILLE. Uh...um...ehhh. Yeah, I guess.

BRENDA. Good. Did you want to say anything first?

ORVILLE. Like what?

BRENDA. Okay, I'll go then. My relationship with my husband isn't evolving.

ORVILLE. You don't have to tell me this.

BRENDA. I know I don't have to. I want to share with you. If afterwards, you want to share with me –

ORVILLE. No.

BRENDA. He doesn't touch me anymore.

ORVILLE. Brenda.

BRENDA. Not really. Not in a real way. If I'm in his way, he'll nudge me aside but when I climb on top of him, he pushes me off. Sometimes when he's sleeping I try to hold his hand but he starts to scream and then he wakes up and is like, "What are you doing?" Like it's my fault he doesn't want to hold my hand.

ORVILLE. Listen, I don't –

BRENDA. I don't expect you to solve my problem for me. I'm not looking for suggestions. It just feels good to talk about it, you know?

ORVILLE. No. I don't know.

BRENDA. I guess when I think about it, my father was never that affectionate. Maybe it's a man thing. Were you affectionate?

ORVILLE. I think I was.

BRENDA. That's nice.

ORVILLE. Not all the time.

BRENDA. No one is all the time. I'm thinking maybe I'll break the television.

ORVILLE. What?

BRENDA. If all he wants to watch is golf, maybe I'll just break the TV. I could even use a golf club. I mean what would he do if I just beat the television with his golf club?

ORVILLE. Go watch it somewhere else?

BRENDA. He's quick to tell me when I'm not meeting his needs, but when I tell him I need a little attention, he just ignores me.

ORVILLE. I'm not really qualified to help you with this.

BRENDA. I'm still attractive, right? Right?

ORVILLE. Yeah.

BRENDA. Are you just saying that?

ORVILLE. No.

BRENDA. Because if you're just saying that…

ORVILLE. I don't know. Maybe you should go out.

BRENDA. What do you mean?

ORVILLE. If you just went out for a drink or something, maybe he'd miss you. No one wants someone needing from them when they're in the middle of something.

BRENDA. That's very wise.

ORVILLE. Actually, *I'm* kind of in the middle of something.

BRENDA. So you want to go out tonight then?

ORVILLE. Oh, no, I didn't mean you and me –

BRENDA. Why not, though?

ORVILLE. You're my boss.

BRENDA. This isn't sexual harassment. Do you feel sexually harassed?

ORVILLE. Um. I do feel like I have some work to do.

BRENDA. It's because of the needy thing, right? Fuck! You think I need you.

ORVILLE. Eh.

BRENDA. I don't want to need from you. I want you to need from me.

ORVILLE. Yeah, uh...that's not – you should just go out with your friends. You have friends?

BRENDA. Do you have friends?

ORVILLE. Not really. Not anymore. I have people who pity me.

BRENDA. I don't pity you.

ORVILLE. You don't?

BRENDA. I mean it's not the main feeling. It's hard not to pity –

ORVILLE. Yeah. Well –

BRENDA. But that's secondary.

ORVILLE. Okay.

BRENDA. If you don't want to go out for a drink, we could have one here after work or in my office.

ORVILLE. I got a baby I have to go home to.

BRENDA. That's right. What's her name?

ORVILLE. Florence.

BRENDA. Really?

ORVILLE. No.

BRENDA. Actually, I have an old bottle of wine in my office. Merlot. You like merlot?

ORVILLE. No.

BRENDA. You want to come back now and we can talk about what we're feeling?

ORVILLE. I can't.

BRENDA. And if you want to cry on my shoulder, I'm up for that. As long as you don't – I'm kind of squeamish, so it's best if we avoid certain topics like involving blood and bones and dying. But I'm not afraid of feelings. You can cry on any part of me. We should probably do it in my office though instead of here in the open. People could get jealous.

ORVILLE. That's okay.

BRENDA. What?

ORVILLE. I don't want to.

BRENDA. You don't want to what?

ORVILLE. Go back to your office and talk about my feelings.

BRENDA. You sure?

ORVILLE. I'm sure.

BRENDA. What if it was a work meeting with wine?

ORVILLE. Will we talk about work?

BRENDA. Sure. Some of the time. Sure.

ORVILLE. No.

BRENDA. Okay. I'll ask you again tomorrow.

Scene Five

(**IAN** *walks across the stage.* **ORVILLE** *sees him and follows him.*)

Scene Six

*(**ORVILLE** talking to the baby. It's late.)*

ORVILLE. Are you awake? Hey, are you awake? Sorry. I know it's late. It's just – I saw the guy who killed your mom. I mean I knew he was out on bail, but I didn't expect to just run into him like that. I don't think he recognized me but I knew it was him right away. Those photographs are burned into my mind.

He was just there all of a sudden. I came out of work and there he was, just walking down twenty-third street, completely free. The nerve of him to be alive while Carrie – so I followed him. I followed him into a grocery store and watched him buy orange juice and coffee. I followed him to his apartment building and I waited outside. Waited so long my legs were tired from standing.

It started to rain. I was about to leave, just forget the whole thing, and then he came out. I followed him into the subway onto the platform. I stood near him while we were waiting for the train. I could have pushed him right into the incoming train. I could have done that then. Instead we both got on the train and when he got off, I got off. We went into this church, down in the basement. It was a meeting for people who were trying not to drink or take drugs anymore. I stood in the back. Am I supposed to feel better that the guy who hit your mother with a car is going to some meeting? Is that supposed to make everything okay somehow? Other people get up and tell their stories but I'm watching him and all I can think is murderer, murderer, murderer.

I'm going to take care of this. This is what I can do. It's his fault you have no mother. It's probably his fault you never cry. I'm going to make sure he's punished for it.

Scene Seven

*(Morning. **WALTER** holding the baby, maybe singing to her. **ORVILLE** enters, putting on his tie.)*

WALTER. When did you get in?

ORVILLE. Sorry.

WALTER. It's fine. It's just – you could have called.

ORVILLE. Sorry. I got wrapped up in something. You didn't have plans? Another date.

WALTER. No, I just... I was expecting you.

ORVILLE. Sorry. I had some things.

WALTER. Oh.

ORVILLE. Went to see a therapist.

WALTER. Oh?

ORVILLE. And then got some drinks.

WALTER. Oh.

ORVILLE. I might have a few more late nights this week.

WALTER. Okay.

ORVILLE. A few things I have to do.

WALTER. Oh?

ORVILLE. For work.

WALTER. Okay.

ORVILLE. Some more therapy.

WALTER. And some more drinking?

ORVILLE. Maybe. People from the office are going out. They invited me along.

WALTER. Just let me know.

ORVILLE. Sure.

WALTER. In case I have plans.

ORVILLE. How did that last date go?

WALTER. She's way too young for me.

ORVILLE. Oh.

WALTER. But she wants to see me again.

ORVILLE. Really?

WALTER. So, I guess I'll do that. I don't know what we'll talk about. Apparently there's a dearth of eligible men.

ORVILLE. Is there?

WALTER. I guess there is.

ORVILLE. So listen, I was thinking, you remember your handgun?

WALTER. What about it?

ORVILLE. Can I borrow it?

WALTER. What for?

ORVILLE. Maybe I'll shoot some rounds off in a shooting range. For therapy.

> (**WALTER** *puts the baby in the bassinet.*)

WALTER. They have guns there.

ORVILLE. You can't take them with you though.

WALTER. I'm not bringing my gun into this house. Not a house with a baby in it.

ORVILLE. No, I could keep it at work. I have a desk drawer that locks.

WALTER. Why?

ORVILLE. I'll drive up and get it.

WALTER. You're going to drive all the way upstate just to get my gun?

ORVILLE. It'll be therapeutic. Just tell me the combination to the safe.

WALTER. What do you want it for?

ORVILLE. Is it mom's birthday?

WALTER. No.

ORVILLE. Is it your birthday?

WALTER. No.

ORVILLE. What is it?

WALTER. Don't drive up there.

ORVILLE. I could just pick it up.

WALTER. What are you doing?

ORVILLE. What do you mean?

WALTER. Why do you want a gun? It's locked up where it is. We don't need to bring it to the city. I don't know what the gun laws are here. I'm not going to bring it here so that you can do, what with it?

ORVILLE. Nothing. Forget it.

WALTER. Are you thinking about suicide? Is this a cry for help? Do I need to worry about you?

ORVILLE. No. God, Dad! No.

WALTER. What is this about? Did something happen?

ORVILLE. Forget it.

WALTER. Tell me what's going on.

ORVILLE. It's nothing. It's just an idea I had. Maybe you're right.

WALTER. Don't do anything stupid. You were never a stupid kid. You never did rash things when you were younger.

ORVILLE. I'm not doing anything.

WALTER. Don't do anything.

ORVILLE. Yeah.

WALTER. Go see your therapist. Come home. Have some sex or whatever.

ORVILLE. I'm not going to –

WALTER. Whatever makes you feel better. And then come home to your baby.

ORVILLE. Yeah.

WALTER. She needs you.

ORVILLE. She doesn't need me.

WALTER. She needs you.

ORVILLE. Yeah.

WALTER. I know you're having a hard time.

ORVILLE. Okay.

WALTER. It'll get better.

ORVILLE. Maybe I need to do something to make it better.

WALTER. Like what?

ORVILLE. I don't know.

WALTER. A gun is not a toy.

ORVILLE. I know.

WALTER. Did you tell the therapist you wanted a gun?

ORVILLE. No. I guess I don't need a gun.

WALTER. Come home after work, okay?

ORVILLE. I'll see if I can.

WALTER. Call me if you're going to be late.

ORVILLE. Yeah.

WALTER. Act like an adult. You're a father now.

ORVILLE. I'm trying.

WALTER. Good.

ORVILLE. I might not do it the way you did it.

WALTER. Whatever you need to do. Just don't do anything stupid.

ORVILLE. I might not be able to avoid that.

WALTER. Try!

Scene Eight

(**ORVILLE** *standing in front of a table that has coffee and doughnuts on it.* **IAN** *comes over, gets himself coffee.* **ORVILLE** *watches him, while unconsciously playing with his wedding ring. After an uncomfortable silence,* **IAN** *sees him.*)

IAN. Hi.

ORVILLE. Oh, hi.

IAN. We haven't met yet. Have we?

ORVILLE. No.

IAN. I'm Ian.

ORVILLE. Hi, Ian. I'm... Ted.

IAN. You're new too?

ORVILLE. Yeah, I guess I am. Did you get up and speak yet?

IAN. No. Not yet. After you get ninety days, you go up.

ORVILLE. I never liked getting up in front of people.

IAN. Yeah. I don't know how I'm going to get through it.

ORVILLE. Yeah, things are still pretty raw for me.

IAN. Me too. Me too. Yeah. Jesus.

ORVILLE. You will go up though? And admit whatever you need to admit?

IAN. Yeah. I'll go up.

ORVILLE. I'm too impatient to wait for the right time for things.

IAN. What can you do?

ORVILLE. I'm going to get out in front of it.

IAN. In front of what?

ORVILLE. It's not important.

IAN. Okay. Well. Good for you.

ORVILLE. I think so too.

IAN. It's good this exists. I always made fun of these things. All the talk about God. But it's helping. Did I see you here the other night?

ORVILLE. Yeah.

IAN. I think you might live in my neighborhood.

ORVILLE. Oh?

IAN. You look familiar.

ORVILLE. I do?

IAN. I've seen you around.

ORVILLE. Right. I think maybe.

IAN. You live in Chelsea?

ORVILLE. Yeah.

IAN. I thought so. We should exchange information.

ORVILLE. Okay.

IAN. If you want.

ORVILLE. Sure.

IAN. Not that I'm planning on falling off the wagon, but if something were to happen...my sponsor lives kind of far away.

ORVILLE. That sounds like a good idea. I can keep an eye on you.

IAN. Right. We'll watch out for each other.

ORVILLE. It's hard to go alone. You married?

IAN. No.

ORVILLE. I was. I never had to go it alone when I had a wife, but now...

IAN. Sorry. Well, if you want to get coffee sometime, outside this room I mean.

ORVILLE. Yeah.

IAN. Okay. Was that weird?

(*Pause.*)

I'm sorry. Just to be clear, I'm not asking you out on a date.

ORVILLE. Oh, good. I mean, I didn't think –

IAN. I didn't think so but I just wanted to make sure. I mean we both live in Chelsea.

ORVILLE. Yeah.

IAN. It's best to be straightforward. I'm trying to be more clear in my communications of my intentions.

ORVILLE. Okay.

IAN. All my old friends are drunks or aren't speaking to me. It's weird to make new friends. It's weird to do everything sober. I can't play pool sober. I thought I could drunk. Now I don't even know. So many things I'm trying to do. It's hard. It's really hard.

(Pause. Sighs.)

We can't change the past.

ORVILLE. No.

IAN. But we can work on the present.

ORVILLE. How do we do that?

IAN. One day at a time.

ORVILLE. What if the way to make things better is unpleasant?

IAN. What do you mean?

ORVILLE. Do you believe in revenge?

IAN. Oh, I don't know. I guess I'm thinking about someday how to forgive myself.

ORVILLE. Oh, don't say that.

IAN. What?

ORVILLE. Forgiving yourself.

IAN. Maybe you're right. Maybe that's too hard.

ORVILLE. Yeah. Forgiving is hard. I'm having a hard time forgiving.

IAN. Oh.

ORVILLE. I think it's because I don't want to.

IAN. Lots of shit happened to lots of people in this room. The program helps. You just have to be open to it.

ORVILLE. I'm not open to it.

IAN. Give it time.

ORVILLE. That's what people keep saying.

IAN. Yeah. I don't know your situation but revenge is never good.

ORVILLE. Sometimes it's good.

IAN. It won't make you feel better.

ORVILLE. Well, I'm not sure how else to make myself feel better. My dad thinks I should go out and have a lot of sex.

IAN. Really?

ORVILLE. But I'm not sure that's a good idea.

IAN. Yeah, I don't know. I'm trying to stay positive. It's hard.

ORVILLE. I can help you. We can talk about it. I'm good at listening.

IAN. That's nice of you.

ORVILLE. We can get that coffee and you can tell me what you're nervous to say in front of all these people. I mean, if you want.

IAN. Maybe. Yeah. Okay. Thanks. It's good to have a support system.

ORVILLE. I guess so.

IAN. It is. We can keep tabs on each other.

ORVILLE. Yeah. I can keep tabs on you.

Scene Nine

(At the office. **ORVILLE** *has a box that he's putting in his desk drawer.* **BRENDA** *enters.)*

BRENDA. What's that?

ORVILLE. Nothing.

BRENDA. You go shopping?

ORVILLE. No.

BRENDA. Is that a gun?

ORVILLE. No. Yeah.

BRENDA. I thought you were at the dentist.

ORVILLE. There was a gun show.

BRENDA. Was this an impulse purchase?

ORVILLE. Yeah. No.

BRENDA. Did you go to Connecticut or somewhere?

ORVILLE. Pennsylvania.

BRENDA. Can I see it?

ORVILLE. I guess.

*(***ORVILLE*** takes it out of the box and hands it to her.)*

BRENDA. Wow. Is it loaded?

ORVILLE. No.

BRENDA. I have to admit. This is pretty fucking sexy. I mean, you shouldn't have this here.

ORVILLE. I know.

BRENDA. HR would freak out.

ORVILLE. Yeah.

BRENDA. You shouldn't have brought it to the office. But damn. It's pretty hot. Don't you think?

ORVILLE. I guess.

BRENDA. Maybe you could get a safety deposit box or something.

ORVILLE. Yeah.

BRENDA. I could hold the key for you if you want. I always wanted to wear a key around my neck.

ORVILLE. No.

BRENDA. You got a permit for this?

ORVILLE. Sure.

BRENDA. I want to go shoot this. We should drive upstate and shoot it.

ORVILLE. Maybe. Um actually, you know what you were talking about?

BRENDA. Hmmm?

ORVILLE. That drink.

BRENDA. We shouldn't drink and shoot firearms. Unless –

ORVILLE. No, I know. I kind of want to shoot it alone.

BRENDA. Oh.

ORVILLE. It's a personal thing.

BRENDA. Isn't everything better with two people?

ORVILLE. This thing maybe is better just for me.

BRENDA. Okay, but –

ORVILLE. I'm going to put the gun away.

BRENDA. Don't do that.

(**ORVILLE** *puts the gun away.*)

BRENDA. Oh, sad. Bye-bye, firearm.

ORVILLE. I was thinking – you want to get a drink?

BRENDA. Really? Tonight?

ORVILLE. If you don't want to...

BRENDA. I want to.

ORVILLE. I don't know what tomorrow holds. So we should get that drink while we have the chance.

BRENDA. Good.

ORVILLE. I mean, you never know.

BRENDA. This is good. I'm so glad you're finally going to open up.

ORVILLE. I didn't say that.

BRENDA. We'll both loosen up. Get comfortable. Have some drinks.

ORVILLE. Yeah.

BRENDA. How about that hotel bar across the street?

ORVILLE. Okay.

BRENDA. Bring the gun. No, wait. Don't bring the gun. Are you going to bring the gun?

ORVILLE. Uh...

BRENDA. I'll leave it up to you. The important thing is that we'll go out.

ORVILLE. Maybe we shouldn't.

BRENDA. You said you wanted to. Don't chicken out on me now.

ORVILLE. I'm not –

BRENDA. You're fragile. I can see that. All the more reason you're careful who you open up to. I am a good person to let in.

ORVILLE. Are you?

BRENDA. I can be very discreet.

ORVILLE. What does that mean?

BRENDA. You look like you need a drink.

ORVILLE. Okay. One drink.

BRENDA. Yes. Maybe two. Let's not count.

ORVILLE. I'm not sure –

BRENDA. This will be fun! You'll see. I'll go change.

      (**BRENDA** *exits.*)

ORVILLE. You don't have to – okay.

Scene Ten

(At the bar, **ORVILLE** *and* **BRENDA** *drink.)*

BRENDA. I like this dress because my legs look good in it. Don't they?

ORVILLE. Sure.

BRENDA. And it clings to me, see?

ORVILLE. Yeah.

BRENDA. It clings so much it makes me feel naked.

ORVILLE. Oh.

BRENDA. You know what I mean?

ORVILLE. I don't have any clothes like that.

BRENDA. Do I look naked?

ORVILLE. No.

BRENDA. Can you imagine me naked?

ORVILLE. Probably.

BRENDA. It's also really easy to clean so if you want I can hold you to my breast and you can cry as much as you want and it'll be totally fine. You want to do that now?

ORVILLE. I don't think so.

BRENDA. Just let me know when. We'll have a few more drinks.

ORVILLE. Okay.

BRENDA. And get loosened up.

ORVILLE. Yeah.

BRENDA. And then you can cry.

ORVILLE. I probably won't do that.

BRENDA. Do you need like a trigger? Should I give you things you can think about? About your wife I mean.

ORVILLE. Don't do that.

BRENDA. It's sad. The way she was killed.

ORVILLE. Please stop.

BRENDA. You can let it all out with me. I will be here for you. I'm an open vessel here to hold your pain and tears.

ORVILLE. Okay.

BRENDA. Don't feel ashamed. You can let your walls down in front of me.

ORVILLE. I don't need to do that.

BRENDA. Don't miss out on opportunities that are being provided for you.

ORVILLE. You think?

BRENDA. Don't live with regrets.

ORVILLE. Yeah. Yeah. I guess. Yeah. Huh.

(*Pause.* **ORVILLE** *thinks.*)

BRENDA. What are you thinking about?

ORVILLE. I'm trying to make a decision.

BRENDA. Can I help? You could tell me what you're thinking about and I could help with pros and cons. We can make a list.

ORVILLE. No.

BRENDA. I'm really good at it. I made a list about tonight.

ORVILLE. What?

BRENDA. Tell me about your dilemma.

ORVILLE. I just, I think I'm about to do something stupid.

BRENDA. Everyone should do stupid things once in a while. Is this a stupid thing I could do with you? It is, isn't it?

ORVILLE. It's not just unwise, or slightly illegal. It's straight up balls to the wall stupid.

BRENDA. Cool.

ORVILLE. And I know this and I think I'm going to do it anyway. Even if it means I end up dead or in jail.

BRENDA. I'm sorry, wait. Is this about us? I had you there and then I lost you.

ORVILLE. Don't worry about it. It's not about you.

BRENDA. I want it to be though. You want me to hold you now? Because I would really like to be held.

ORVILLE. I think I should go.

BRENDA. No, don't go. Nothing happened.

ORVILLE. Yeah, I know. That's why it would be a good time
to go now.

   (**BRENDA** *grabs him, kisses him.*)

BRENDA. There. Okay? Now you can stay.

ORVILLE. Brenda, I...

BRENDA. No. I don't want objections. You can cry. We can
talk. We can kiss. But no objections.

   (*They kiss again.*)

ORVILLE. No. I can't do this. I'm sorry.

BRENDA. Wait, where are you going? Don't desert me!!

   (**ORVILLE** *exits.*)

Scene Eleven

(**ORVILLE** *over the bassinet, late at night.*)

ORVILLE. I should tell you about your mother. What can I say? You'll have pictures. There will always be photos for you to look at when you're growing up. But you'll wonder about her and that's understandable. The first thing you should know is that she was funny. She was beautiful, of course. You can see that. But she was also kind of goofy. She never cared what people thought. If she thought it was funny to walk on her toes for a while, she would walk around like that all day. She was always making faces at kids she saw on the train, sticking her tongue out at them when their parents weren't looking. They loved it. Your childhood would have been a lot of fun with her. She would have built forts with you. She would have done anything for you. And then when you got older – she's a really smart woman. She would give you great advice. Her advice would be – your teens would be easy with a mom like that. She would have…

It doesn't make sense that I'm here and she's gone. She would have been a great mother. And I'm just… I'm sorry.

Your grandfather can take care of you. He did a good job with me, mostly. And he'll say nice things about me probably when you ask about your parents. Will you? Ask about us?

Scene Twelve

(Church basement. A table with coffee and doughnuts. **IAN** *and* **ORVILLE** *stand there drinking coffee.* **ORVILLE** *has his coat on. There shouldn't be a bulge or anything to imply a gun, but* **ORVILLE** *is hiding it under his coat.)*

IAN. Aren't you hot?

ORVILLE. I'm fine.

IAN. You don't need to keep your coat on.

ORVILLE. I'm comfortable.

IAN. It's good to see you again.

ORVILLE. Yeah?

IAN. I actually almost called you a couple of times. About that coffee. But then I didn't.

ORVILLE. Okay.

IAN. Should I have called?

ORVILLE. Yeah.

IAN. I just didn't want to drag you down. I'm in a really bad place right now.

ORVILLE. Me too.

IAN. I mean, you know what they say. Misery loves –

ORVILLE. Coffee.

IAN. Right. Yeah.

ORVILLE. We could get coffee right after, if you want.

IAN. Okay.

ORVILLE. Or go somewhere else and talk. Somewhere quiet. Isolated.

IAN. We could go to my place.

ORVILLE. That sounds like a good idea.

IAN. Wait, I'm sorry. This still isn't a date. Did that sound like a date?

ORVILLE. No.

IAN. It kinda sounded like a date to me.

ORVILLE. No. We're just hanging out.

IAN. Right.

ORVILLE. I'll come over and we'll hang out. Right after.

IAN. Cool.

ORVILLE. So that will happen. We can hang out together, alone. That's perfect.

>   *(Suddenly terrified.)*

Oh, fuck.

IAN. What?

ORVILLE. Nothing.

IAN. You have somewhere else you have to be?

ORVILLE. No.

IAN. You sure?

ORVILLE. Yeah.

IAN. You know, it's probably better if I don't drag you down, though.

ORVILLE. Are you trying to break the plans we just made?

IAN. I'm just in a bad place.

ORVILLE. You think you're in a worse place than me?

IAN. I probably am.

ORVILLE. You don't know.

IAN. I know, but –

ORVILLE. You don't know.

IAN. Right, but –

ORVILLE. Fuck you!

IAN. What?

ORVILLE. Fuck you for being so self centered you can't see anyone else. Fuck you, buddy! What you're going through is nothing like what I'm going through. You can go fuck yourself.

IAN. No, I –

ORVILLE. No. Fuck you! Fuck you! Fuck you!

>   *(**ORVILLE** leaves.)*

Scene Thirteen

(**ORVILLE**'s *desk at work.* **ORVILLE** *works.*
BRENDA *approaches.*)

BRENDA. Hi cutie.

ORVILLE. Don't call me that.

BRENDA. But you're cute, cutie. What else would I call you?

ORVILLE. Don't call me anything.

BRENDA. Orville?

ORVILLE. Okay, you can call me that.

BRENDA. Sweetheart.

ORVILLE. No.

BRENDA. I'm mad at you.

ORVILLE. Okay.

BRENDA. The way you ran out of our meeting.

ORVILLE. What meeting?

BRENDA. At the bar. You were bad. Bad!

ORVILLE. Mmm hmm.

BRENDA. It's possible I'm partially to blame. I may have come on too strong.

ORVILLE. Did you?

BRENDA. I may have. My energy may have spooked you.

ORVILLE. Spooked? I'm not a bunny rabbit.

BRENDA. You kind of are though. And I accept responsibility for scaring you away. Are you willing to accept your responsibility?

ORVILLE. For what?

BRENDA. Running from your feelings?

ORVILLE. I'm not running from my feelings.

BRENDA. You're not? Aren't you? Aren't you?

ORVILLE. Maybe.

BRENDA. Orville, Orville, Orville.

ORVILLE. Brenda.

BRENDA. You can't run from your pain.

ORVILLE. I know.

BRENDA. I see you trying. It won't work. You need to run to something, not away from something. And I can be that something.

ORVILLE. Which something?

BRENDA. The running to something.

ORVILLE. You're right.

BRENDA. Yes.

ORVILLE. About me running. I'm chicken shit.

BRENDA. No. Uh.

ORVILLE. Something needs to be done and I'm not man enough to do it.

BRENDA. Okay. Well, the working day is almost done. My little clock says we could go out and have another meeting.

ORVILLE. But I can be that man. Right?

BRENDA. What?

ORVILLE. I can take care of what needs taking care of. It's in me.

BRENDA. What's in you?

ORVILLE. If I had been born at another time I would have been drafted to fight in a war. Then I would have known what I was made of. I don't have that, but I have this instead.

BRENDA. What?

ORVILLE. It's been nice working with you.

BRENDA. Why are you saying that?

ORVILLE. I mean most of the time. The point is, I don't dislike you.

BRENDA. Excuse me?

ORVILLE. I have to go do something and you may never see me again. Goodbye, Brenda.

      (**ORVILLE** *exits.*)

BRENDA. No, wait. Hold on. We need to have a meeting!

Scene Fourteen

(**WALTER** *and* **ORVILLE**. **ORVILLE** *doesn't wear his coat.* **WALTER** *holds the baby.*)

WALTER. You're going to AA?

ORVILLE. Yeah.

WALTER. Well, if that's what you think you need.

ORVILLE. Yeah.

WALTER. Except that you still come home smelling of alcohol.

ORVILLE. I haven't gotten to that step yet.

WALTER. The step where you stop drinking? I think that's the first step.

ORVILLE. I just started going. I'm easing into it.

WALTER. I guess.

ORVILLE. Anyway, so that's what I'm doing with my nights.

WALTER. Okay.

ORVILLE. I'm seeking out my demons.

WALTER. Okay.

ORVILLE. You don't have to say "okay" like that.

WALTER. How would you like for me to say it?

ORVILLE. Okay.

WALTER. Okay.

ORVILLE. Okay.

WALTER. Okay.

ORVILLE. Okay.

WALTER. Okay. I think Pudding had her first crush.

ORVILLE. What?

WALTER. Today she saw another baby. A boy. And she smiled. Sort of smiled. And stared.

ORVILLE. Oh.

WALTER. So I guess she's straight.

ORVILLE. Okay.

WALTER. I'm kidding.

ORVILLE. Yeah.

WALTER. That was a joke.

ORVILLE. Right. Don't call her Pudding.

WALTER. Okay.

ORVILLE. Call her...something else.

WALTER. Okay.

ORVILLE. Are you still getting phone numbers? At the park?

WALTER. Oh. A couple. I'm waiting. Until you're better.

ORVILLE. Sorry.

WALTER. No. I'm waiting. I can be patient.

ORVILLE. I have trouble with patience.

WALTER. I know. You always have. It's gotten better. When you were a kid –

ORVILLE. I know.

WALTER. I think Pudding takes after me. She has a lot of patience.

ORVILLE. That's good.

WALTER. Not that it's too late. It's still something you can acquire. A little at a time.

ORVILLE. Maybe.

WALTER. Don't say it like that.

ORVILLE. Like what?

WALTER. Maybe.

ORVILLE. Maybe.

WALTER. Maybe.

ORVILLE. Maybe.

WALTER. I think being a father taught me a lot of patience. It'll do that for you too.

ORVILLE. Yeah?

WALTER. Once you're ready.

ORVILLE. Maybe.

WALTER. I trust you, you know.

ORVILLE. Don't say that.

WALTER. You always had a good head on your shoulders.

ORVILLE. Stop.

WALTER. Even when you lacked patience.

ORVILLE. I got to go now.

WALTER. Okay. Godspeed.

ORVILLE. Yeah. Listen, I just want to tell you, you were a really good father.

WALTER. Oh.

ORVILLE. A much better father than I could ever be.

WALTER. No.

ORVILLE. I'm really lucky to have you. And the baby is too.

WALTER. We're lucky to have you.

ORVILLE. Don't say that.

WALTER. We're lucky to have you.

ORVILLE. I – I have to go. Bye, Pudding. Fuck, you got me doing it too.

(**ORVILLE** *exits.* **WALTER** *looks where he left.*)

WALTER. What is he doing? Should we worry? At a certain point you have to let them go. Huh, Pudding? And just hope for the best.

Scene Fifteen

*(In **IAN**'s apartment. A couch. **ORVILLE** wears his coat. **IAN** leads him in.)*

IAN. I didn't expect to see you again.

ORVILLE. Yeah, I was upset.

IAN. You were really upset.

ORVILLE. Probably I could have – I was a scared piece of shit.

IAN. It's not a competition, you know.

ORVILLE. I know.

IAN. We can both be having a hard time.

ORVILLE. Yeah. I'm just angry.

IAN. Do you want to talk about it?

ORVILLE. I'm not going to cry on your shoulder.

IAN. I'm not saying you should. But it wouldn't be wrong if you did.

ORVILLE. I'm not going to do that.

IAN. Okay.

ORVILLE. People need to stop trying to get me to do that.

IAN. Sorry. I just thought it would be helpful. Maybe I'm projecting.

ORVILLE. You mean you want to cry on my shoulder?

IAN. No. I mean I don't have to do that.

ORVILLE. What do you have to cry about?

IAN. I don't have to cry.

ORVILLE. You must have things to cry about.

IAN. You don't want to hear about it.

ORVILLE. I do.

IAN. No, it's...nothing.

ORVILLE. What do you mean nothing? It was nothing?

IAN. You don't want to hear.

ORVILLE. Try me.

IAN. No.

ORVILLE. *(Stern.)* Try me.

>*(Pause.)*

IAN. I made a mistake.

ORVILLE. What kind of mistake?

IAN. A stupid one. When I drank sometimes I felt powerful. It was the only time I ever felt that way and it would cause me to do things I otherwise wouldn't do.

ORVILLE. Like what?

IAN. Unprotected sex. Fistfights. Drugs.

ORVILLE. So you –

IAN. I mean I made a lot of bad decisions. And because of one of them, I might go to jail.

ORVILLE. You might?

IAN. Yeah.

ORVILLE. What did you do?

IAN. I was driving my friend's car. Drunk. There was an accident. People got hurt.

ORVILLE. Got hurt.

IAN. Yeah.

ORVILLE. But no one died.

IAN. Someone...died.

ORVILLE. Who?

IAN. A woman.

ORVILLE. And you feel bad?

IAN. I feel terrible.

ORVILLE. That's not enough.

IAN. What?

ORVILLE. You just feel really bad?

IAN. What do you mean?

ORVILLE. What are you going to do?

IAN. It's my first DUI. My lawyer says maybe... You know what, we don't need to talk about this.

ORVILLE. Your lawyer thinks he can get you off?

IAN. Well, he didn't say that exactly.

ORVILLE. What did he say?

IAN. I don't really want to talk about this now.

ORVILLE. He can get you off?

IAN. Probably not. I'm kind of terrified.

ORVILLE. Okay.

IAN. But I guess I have to pay my debt.

ORVILLE. Your debt? You think that will pay off your debt?

IAN. I don't know. I don't want to go to jail.

ORVILLE. But you will go to jail? For sure?

IAN. Let's not talk about that.

ORVILLE. I kind of want to talk about that.

IAN. What about you? Are you seeing anyone?

ORVILLE. Why does everyone keep asking me that?

IAN. Who's asking you?

ORVILLE. Everyone thinks I should be having sex.

IAN. Should you?

ORVILLE. No, probably not. It's too soon.

IAN. Right.

ORVILLE. But no one seems to get that. My boss kissed me.

IAN. Really? That's crazy. Was there tongue?

ORVILLE. Ha!

IAN. Was there groping? Some sweaty passion in the copy room?

ORVILLE. Ha. No.

IAN. Bent over the water cooler

ORVILLE. *(Catching himself.)* Don't do that.

IAN. What?

ORVILLE. You're trying to make me like you.

IAN. You don't want to like me?

ORVILLE. That sounded weird, huh?

IAN. I wish I had a drink right now. It makes these kinds of moments easier.

ORVILLE. What kind of moments?

> (**IAN** *leans over and kisses him.*)

ORVILLE. Oh.

IAN. I'm sorry. Did I misread that?

ORVILLE. Yeah.

IAN. Yeah?

ORVILLE. I mean, yeah.

IAN. Okay.

ORVILLE. That's not why I'm here. I'm not here for that.

IAN. I'm sorry. I'm so stupid. I thought –

ORVILLE. Can I have a drink or something?

IAN. Yeah. Of course. What do you want?

ORVILLE. What do you have?

> (**IAN** *exits to the kitchen, out of sight.*)

IAN. I have some soda and water. Orange juice. I could make coffee.

ORVILLE. Coffee.

> (**ORVILLE** *takes out his handgun.*)

IAN. I'll just make a pot.

> (**ORVILLE** *picks up a pillow from the couch, holds it in front of the gun, like a silencer. He aims the gun in the direction* **IAN** *left, as if to shoot him when he returns.*)

I feel like such a fucking idiot. You come over looking for a friend and I'm... I guess I thought... I've always had this problem. It's not just you. Sometimes you see the signals you want to see instead of the signals that are actually there. I used to ask. I used to say, "Can I kiss you now?" but it's so unromantic. So unspontaneous. I just thought... But yeah. Sorry about that. I guess I needed you to want that whether or not you did. I guess I just really need something right now. This whole thing has been really fucked up. Not just being sober, but... I was a whole different person. I never thought I'd be the kind of person who – it's been really hard to get through the day. I stopped drinking because I had to. I couldn't keep going that way but now I'm trying to figure out how to keep living, you know?

I'm running out of reasons to stay alive. Not that – I'm sorry. This isn't your problem. You don't want to hear this. Right? Ted? Are you still there?

ORVILLE. I'm still here.

IAN. You don't have to stay.

ORVILLE. There's something I have to do.

IAN. Okay. Do you want the coffee, or...

ORVILLE. I'm just thinking.

IAN. Okay.

ORVILLE. We have to live with the consequences of our actions.

IAN. Yeah.

ORVILLE. You and me both.

IAN. Yeah.

ORVILLE. As long as we keep living.

IAN. Yeah. That's what I've been thinking about. Why am I alive? I don't mean to put this on you. I'm sorry. I should probably come back in the room. It's just easier not to face you after what just happened. But I guess the easier way isn't always... I'll be out in a minute. I'm sorry. I'm so stupid. I guess I just wanted to forget for a minute.

ORVILLE. Yeah. Right. Forget.

IAN. I'll be out.

ORVILLE. Wait.

IAN. What?

ORVILLE. Not yet.

IAN. I'm sorry?

ORVILLE. Stay there.

IAN. But –

ORVILLE. I'm just not ready yet.

IAN. But I can't keep hiding.

(**ORVILLE** *exits.*)

(**IAN** *enters. Sees* **ORVILLE** *has gone.*)

Scene Sixteen

(*Hotel room.* **ORVILLE** *and* **BRENDA** *drinking wine.*)

BRENDA. I was so surprised when you called.

ORVILLE. Yeah.

BRENDA. It was a good surprise. The way you left today, I didn't know what to think. Is everything okay?

ORVILLE. No.

BRENDA. Tell me about it.

ORVILLE. No.

BRENDA. I'm here for you. How many times do I have to tell you I'm here for you?

ORVILLE. I don't want to talk.

BRENDA. Cry then.

ORVILLE. I don't want to cry.

BRENDA. Okay.

ORVILLE. I want to forget.

BRENDA. What do you mean?

(**ORVILLE** *kisses her.*)

Oh.

(*They kiss for a while and then begin removing each others' clothing.*)

ORVILLE. Wait, hold on.

BRENDA. Don't stop.

(*She kisses him. He gets back into it. More clothes come off. Then they are making love. This goes on just a little too long for the subscriber base.*)

ORVILLE. (*Coming.*) Aaaaah!

BRENDA. Wow.

ORVILLE. Uuh.

BRENDA. Yeah.

(Whoever's on top rolls off. They lie next to one another.)

BRENDA. That was surprising.

ORVILLE. What did I just do? What the fuck did I just do?

BRENDA. I'll tell you what you did.

ORVILLE. No. No. No. It's all wrong. You're the wrong size, the wrong shape.

BRENDA. No.

ORVILLE. I just want my wife.

BRENDA. Shhh.

ORVILLE. I just want my wife.

BRENDA. Come on.

ORVILLE. I want my wife. I want my wife. I want my wife. I want my wife.

BRENDA. I'm here. Brenda is here for you.

ORVILLE. I want my wife!

BRENDA. Come on.

ORVILLE. Carrie! Carrie!

BRENDA. Stop.

ORVILLE. I want my wife!

> **(ORVILLE** *cries on her, shaking, hyperventilating maybe. It's not pretty. She takes it all, uncertainly. She's trying but she's out of her depth.)*

BRENDA. Shh. I can be enough for you.

ORVILLE. No. I loved her. Do you know what love is?

BRENDA. Yes.

ORVILLE. You don't. You never had what I had. If you had what I had, you would understand.

BRENDA. I know what love is.

ORVILLE. No, you don't. No one else does.

BRENDA. I know what it is.

ORVILLE. You don't. You don't.

BRENDA. I know what love is!

Scene Seventeen

(Back at **ORVILLE**'s *place.* **WALTER** *holds the baby while reading her a children's book.)*

WALTER. And then when the four bears in the ant costumes finished cleaning the house, they took their mops and brushes and waved goodbye. Timmy smiled, because he knew that if not for the four bear-ants his mother never would have forgiven him.

*(***ORVILLE** *enters. His father looks up.)*

Oh, look, Pudding. Your father's home.

ORVILLE. I slept with her.

WALTER. What?

ORVILLE. I slept with her.

WALTER. Let me put Pudding down.

*(***WALTER** *exits with the baby.* **ORVILLE** *gets a beer.* **WALTER** *re-enters. He looks at the beer in* **ORVILLE**'s *hand but says nothing.)*

So –

ORVILLE. When I was married, I always wondered what it would be like to have sex with other women.

WALTER. Sure.

ORVILLE. You think that's what you want. Of course that's what you want.

WALTER. Yeah.

ORVILLE. But it was just wrong.

WALTER. I know.

ORVILLE. How do you know?

WALTER. It took me a while after your mother passed.

ORVILLE. Really?

WALTER. Sure. We were together a long time. You know how many times we probably had sex in forty-three years?

ORVILLE. I don't want to think about that.

WALTER. I'm just saying I understand what you're saying. It felt like cheating the first time I slept with another woman.

ORVILLE. Yeah.

WALTER. You assume that you'll like something new and different, but when you have it –

ORVILLE. I know.

WALTER. It gets easier.

ORVILLE. Okay.

WALTER. Sex will become fun again. I promise. You just need time. Nowadays I have the kind of sex I never imagined. In public sometimes. Crazy positions. I'm like a kid.

ORVILLE. I'm glad but again, really, let's not talk about your sex life.

WALTER. I never talked to you about sex.

ORVILLE. What?

WALTER. When you were growing up, I was too embarrassed.

ORVILLE. Oh. That's okay.

WALTER. I don't get embarrassed now that I'm old.

ORVILLE. You're not old.

WALTER. Anyway, if you ever –

ORVILLE. I don't need to talk to you about sex.

WALTER. Sure, but...

ORVILLE. Really. I'm fine.

WALTER. Things will get better.

ORVILLE. They will?

WALTER. I promise.

ORVILLE. And the pain stops?

WALTER. It never stops really. But it's less immediate. If it stopped it wasn't really love.

ORVILLE. I want it to stop.

WALTER. Someday you'll miss it.

ORVILLE. I can't imagine that.

WALTER. It's good to talk to you again. I thought I'd lost you there for a bit.

ORVILLE. Oh. Yeah. I'm not sure I've been found yet.

WALTER. What do you think about Lily?

ORVILLE. Who's Lily?

WALTER. For a name. For Pudding.

ORVILLE. No.

WALTER. Gertrude?

ORVILLE. No.

WALTER. Marcie.

ORVILLE. Stop.

WALTER. Not ready?

ORVILLE. We'll do it later.

WALTER. Okay.

ORVILLE. We'll do it later.

WALTER. When?

ORVILLE. I don't know, Dad. Later, okay?

WALTER. Okay.

Scene Eighteen

(The office. **ORVILLE** *is at his desk.* **BRENDA**
rushes by.)

ORVILLE. Brenda!

BRENDA. Can't stop now. A million things to do before the end of the day. Busy times!

ORVILLE. *(Standing.)* Wait! Please.

(**BRENDA** *comes back over.)*

BRENDA. Make it quick. I only have a second. Is it about the Hartwell report?

ORVILLE. No.

BRENDA. I don't have time. What is it?

ORVILLE. I just wanted to say...

BRENDA. What?

ORVILLE. About last night.

BRENDA. *(Lying.)* I don't know what you're talking about.

ORVILLE. Our business meeting.

BRENDA. Oh, well. I hope I set you straight on your accounts.

ORVILLE. I needed that. It was –

BRENDA. Okay. Talk to you later.

ORVILLE. I'm sorry if it was awkward after.

BRENDA. I don't know what you mean.

ORVILLE. I said some things. I know it wasn't normal pillow talk.

BRENDA. I'm a married woman.

ORVILLE. I guess –

BRENDA. I'm a happily married woman.

ORVILLE. Of course.

BRENDA. My husband would not want you to talk like this. I'm married.

ORVILLE. Okay.

BRENDA. To a man I love.

ORVILLE. Okay.

BRENDA. And he does not deserve you talking like this.

ORVILLE. Okay, but –

BRENDA. He deserves my devotion. Because if anything were to happen to him –

ORVILLE. Nothing will happen to him.

BRENDA. Can you say that?

ORVILLE. Well –

BRENDA. You don't know. If there's anything I've learned from what happened to you, it's that no one can say what could happen. *(Softening.)* I'm sorry. Was that insensitive?

ORVILLE. I'm okay.

BRENDA. Good. Well, I just wanted to be clear on where we stand on the past and on the future. This is a place of business. I am your boss. Nothing more. If you need some emotional help, get the name of a psychologist from HR.

ORVILLE. I probably won't do that.

BRENDA. It's nothing personal. We're colleagues.

ORVILLE. Yeah.

BRENDA. *(Softening.)* I understand you're going through a hard time.

ORVILLE. Yeah.

BRENDA. If we can do anything.

ORVILLE. No, that's okay.

BRENDA. Just ask.

ORVILLE. I'm fine.

BRENDA. Good, well, I'll expect that report then.

ORVILLE. Okay well, we don't have to ever talk about it again if that's what you want, but I did want to say thank you. So, thanks. It actually kind of meant a lot to me.

BRENDA. Um, well, okay.

ORVILLE. I know I said some things, but I didn't mean to hurt you. That was about me, not you. And I wanted to say. Your husband's a lucky man.

BRENDA. *(Flustered.)* Really? Okay, well, okay. Thanks. Keep up the good work. I'll – I'll expect that report.

> (**BRENDA** *exits.* **ORVILLE** *gets back to work. His cell phone rings.*)

ORVILLE. Hello?

Scene Nineteen

(**IAN**'s *apartment.* **IAN** *is opening the door for* **ORVILLE**. **ORVILLE** *enters.* **IAN** *is drunk.*)

IAN. Come in. Come in. Come in.

ORVILLE. Are you drunk?

IAN. Maybe I am. So, you're here. That's something. You want a drink. Oh, probably not, huh?

ORVILLE. I'll have a drink.

IAN. No, no.

ORVILLE. Give me a drink.

IAN. No.

ORVILLE. Give me a drink.

(**IAN** *pours him a drink.*)

IAN. So thanks for coming.

ORVILLE. Yeah.

IAN. I didn't think you would after –

ORVILLE. Yeah.

IAN. But I did call you here. The reason I called you – I'm gonna kill myself.

(*Pause.*)

ORVILLE. And you want me to stop you?

IAN. Yeah. I mean there are reasons not to, right?

ORVILLE. There are always reasons not to do anything.

IAN. So what are those reasons?

ORVILLE. Who says you shouldn't do it?

IAN. You think I should do it?

ORVILLE. If it's important to you –

IAN. It is, kind of. But I'm depressed and fucked up.

ORVILLE. Sure.

IAN. Tell me why I should keep living. Tell me about rainbows and sunlight and shit.

ORVILLE. Are you alive for rainbows?

IAN. I don't know. I mean, there must be a reason, right?

ORVILLE. Well, how were you planning on doing it?

(**IAN** *shows him the bottle.*)

IAN. Sleeping pills.

ORVILLE. What if you wake up?

IAN. I'll take a lot.

ORVILLE. That could work.

IAN. Yeah.

ORVILLE. But it might not. I have a better way.

(**ORVILLE** *takes out his gun.*)

IAN. Where did that come from?

ORVILLE. I've been carrying it around. I was going to – but no, you can shoot yourself if you want.

IAN. It's loaded?

ORVILLE. Yeah.

IAN. I think I just sobered up.

(**IAN** *downs the rest of his drink and pours another.*)

Aren't you supposed to talk me out of killing myself instead of bringing me a gun?

ORVILLE. It's what you want, isn't it?

IAN. Yes.

ORVILLE. Tell me why.

IAN. I can't live with myself.

ORVILLE. Sounds like a good reason to me.

IAN. Just like that?

ORVILLE. Just like that.

IAN. Maybe I should call a hotline or something.

ORVILLE. They'll just try to talk you out of it.

IAN. Yeah.

ORVILLE. You don't need that.

IAN. If it's such a good idea, more people would do it though, right?

ORVILLE. It takes bravery.

IAN. I guess.

ORVILLE. Do you have that?

IAN. It takes bravery to stay alive too, right?

ORVILLE. No. Everyone fucking does that.

IAN. Yeah. I don't know.

ORVILLE. You hate yourself, right?

IAN. Yeah.

ORVILLE. You don't think you deserve to live.

IAN. Yeah.

ORVILLE. Well, you're probably right.

IAN. But –

ORVILLE. Can you tell me you think you deserve to live?

IAN. No.

ORVILLE. Okay, so that's where we are.

IAN. So I should just. I guess I can just – you probably don't want to be around for this.

ORVILLE. I need to be here.

IAN. Okay.

ORVILLE. For moral support.

IAN. Maybe I should write a note.

ORVILLE. Okay. Who are you writing the note to? I mean who's gonna read it? Your sponsor? Your mother?

IAN. My parents are dead.

ORVILLE. *(Sincere.)* I'm sorry.

IAN. Most of my family isn't talking to me.

ORVILLE. So who's it for?

IAN. I don't know. It just seems like the thing to do.

ORVILLE. I don't want to lose momentum here. Are we going to get caught up on this letter thing?

IAN. I just want to do it right.

(**IAN** *opens a laptop.*)

ORVILLE. All right. So we'll write a note. You want to dictate?

(**ORVILLE** *sits at the laptop.*)

IAN. To Whom It May Concern:

ORVILLE. I mean, that's a little impersonal.

IAN. Yeah. To A Possible Sympathetic Soul,

ORVILLE. Okay.

IAN. I've made a lot of mistakes in my life. I've lied to a lot of people who were close to me. I let a lot of people down, over and over. I just wanted to say, before I go... that I'm sorry.

ORVILLE. You're sorry.

IAN. I hope you can find it in your heart to forgive me, but even if you don't, I'm sure you'll find peace after I'm gone. It's clear the world will be a better place without me in it.

ORVILLE. Okay.

IAN. And the pain of living my life will finally be over. I don't know if you'll ever read this. I don't know who still cares enough to find out. Let me just say you will no longer have to worry about me fucking up. My fucking up days are over. Sincerely,

ORVILLE. Sincerely,

IAN. How was that?

(*Pause.*)

ORVILLE. That will work.

IAN. Let me see.

(**IAN** *reads it over.* **ORVILLE** *watches him.*)

Yeah.

(**IAN** *types his name.*)

ORVILLE. So that's done.

IAN. Yeah. Okay. So I guess. I guess. Maybe I should do it... right now?

ORVILLE. It's probably best if you shoot yourself in the head. You want me to do it?

IAN. No. Wait. Okay. Wait. Okay. Give me the gun.

(**ORVILLE** *points the gun at him.*)

ORVILLE. Open your mouth.

> (**IAN** *does.* **ORVILLE** *puts the barrel in his mouth.*)

Before we do this, I think I should probably tell you something. My name isn't Ted. My name is Orville Marks.

> (**IAN** *tries to talk but has difficulty because of the gun in his mouth.*)

IAN. Marks?

ORVILLE. It was my wife you hit with your fucking car. She just went out to get milk. It should have been me you hit instead. We had an argument. It was a long day and I had just come home and she was like, "Can you go to the store?" and I yelled at her like an asshole. She said, "Fine, I'll do it." I should have stopped her. But I was a lazy piece of shit and I let her walk out the door with her big swollen belly. If it had been me, maybe I could have got out of the way when you ran the red light. She couldn't move as fast because she was carrying our child. Or maybe not. Maybe I'd be dead too. Either way, it should have been me. But it wasn't. So now I'm here with this gun.

> (*Beat.*)

So what do you have to say for yourself?

IAN. (*Gun in mouth.*) Do it.

> (**ORVILLE** *takes the gun out.*)

ORVILLE. What?

IAN. Do it. Kill me. Do it.

> (**ORVILLE** *points the gun at* **IAN**'s *head. He cocks the hammer. They stand there like that for a long time looking at each other. Finally,* **ORVILLE** *lowers the gun.*)

ORVILLE. Give me your sleeping pills.

*(**IAN** hands them over. **ORVILLE** pockets them.)*

ORVILLE. I'm not going to shoot you.

IAN. But –

ORVILLE. I want you to live with what you did.

IAN. No.

ORVILLE. You have to live with it.

IAN. I can't.

ORVILLE. I want you to. You owe it to me. Promise me. In jail, out of jail, whatever. Every day for the rest of your life I want you to remember how you killed my wife, the mother of my child, and how I didn't shoot you in the head.

IAN. Okay.

ORVILLE. I'm going to check up on you.

IAN. Okay.

ORVILLE. I'm gonna – I don't know what I'm going to do.

IAN. I'm sorry.

ORVILLE. Yeah.

IAN. I'm sorry.

ORVILLE. I know.

IAN. I'm sorry.

ORVILLE. Shut up.

IAN. I'm sorry.

ORVILLE. Shut your mouth.

IAN. I'm sorry.

*(**ORVILLE** points the gun at him.)*

ORVILLE. Shut the fuck up.

IAN. I'm sorry.

ORVILLE. I know.

IAN. Thank you.

*(**ORVILLE** nods, exits.)*

Scene Twenty

(**ORVILLE** *before the bassinet.*)

ORVILLE. I went to the river and I tossed all his pills in. Then I threw the gun in. Someday I'll ask you if I made the right choice. Right now, I have to make decisions for both of us. I don't know. I guess I'll be second guessing everything now that I'm a father. So, what do you think, Angela? No? Lisa? No? Susan? No? Allegra? No? Sylvia? No? Barbara? No? Heather?

(*Pause.*)

Heather it is.

(**WALTER** *enters.*)

Her name is Heather.

WALTER. Heather! Hi Heather! I like it.

ORVILLE. Good.

WALTER. How's everything going?

ORVILLE. It's okay.

WALTER. Good.

(**WALTER** *picks up the baby.*)

How do you like your name, Heather? Do you like it? Here, you take her.

ORVILLE. No, I... Okay.

(**ORVILLE** *takes the baby. She begins to cry.* **WALTER** *and* **ORVILLE** *look at each other, excited.*)

WALTER. She's crying!

ORVILLE. I know. What do I do?

WALTER. You'll know what to do.

ORVILLE. (*To* **HEATHER.**) It's okay. It's going to be okay. Everything's going to be okay.

End of Play